THIS BOOK BELONGS TO:

OTHER MY FRIEND PARIS BOOKS

Published by:

New Year Publishing, LLC   144 Diablo Ranch Ct.   Danville, CA 94506 USA

orders@newyearpublishing.com   http://www.newyearpublishing.com

© 2009 by New Year Publishing, LLC All rights reserved.

Library of Congress Control Number: 2009ZZZ278

ISBN: 978-0979988585

NEW YEAR
PUBLISHING, LLC.

Paris Goes to Lake Tahoe

By Paris Morris

I love going to Lake Tahoe with my family. Lake Tahoe is in the mountains, three hours from our house.

We always pickup a pie at Ikeda's on the way. My Daddy's favorite is Dutch apple.

We have a contest to see who can first spot the Olympic Rings at the entrance to Squaw Valley.

In the winter we snow ski. I love being on the ski team and racing with my friends.

When my cousins Jenna and Sarah come to visit
we go snowboarding. Our instructor Danielle is
always so nice and makes it so much fun.

My sisters love making a snowman.

Our Aunt Michelle got
us snowball makers.

Sometimes we drive to Reno to see all of the light.
At night, downtown Reno is lit up as bright as day.

In the summer we go boating on the lake with Uncle Barry and Aunt Kristen. I like being pulled by the boat in the big tube.

My Dad brings us with him to play golf sometimes.

We usually meet our friends Saryan
and Sierra for dinner in Truckee.

We make s'mores at the firepit in The Village.
My Mom likes her marshmallows burnt.

Rafting down the
Truckee River is one of
the best parts of the
summer. The river runs
just fast enough to
make it exciting.

On the 4th of July the big
fireworks go off over the lake.
We watch from the beach.

We also spend a lot of time
in the swimming pool.

Lake Tahoe is one of my favorite places to go with my family.

CPSIA information can be obtained
at www.ICGtesting.com
233756LV00001B